ELMER
and ROSE

David McKee

Andersen Press

For Big David M

This American edition published in 2012 for Books are Fun by Andersen Press Ltd.,
20 Vauxhall Bridge Road, London SW1V 2SA.
Text and Illustration copyright © David McKee, 2005
The rights of David McKee to be identified as the author and illustrator
of this work have been asserted by him in accordance with
the Copyright, Designs and Patents Act, 1988.
All rights reserved.
British Library Cataloguing in Publication Data available.

Color separated in Switzerland by Photolitho AG, Zürich.
Manufactured in China by C & C Offset Printing Co., Ltd.
1-C&C-6/26/12

ISBN 978 1 84939 550 2

A young friend of Elmer's named Rose
Blushes from her head to her toes,
Or sometimes instead
From her toes to her head
But never from her tail to her nose.

Elmer, the patchwork elephant, was with his cousin
Wilbur. They were looking at the herd of elephants.
"Jolly fellows," smiled Wilbur, "but not exactly unique."
"They're all unique," said Elmer. "Just not as different as
us. Imagine a herd like you or me."

At that moment, Bird arrived and said,
"Grandpa Eldo wants you two."
"Come on, Wilbur," said Elmer.

Grandpa Eldo was looking under a bush.
"Where is she?" he muttered.
Then, seeing Elmer and Wilbur, he said,
"She must be hiding from you two."
"She?" said Elmer. "Who are you talking about?"

"Rose," said Eldo. "She wandered away from a herd
of elephants that passed nearby. You two can take her
back to them. Ah! There she is. Don't be frightened,
Rose. Come and meet Elmer and Wilbur."

From behind a tree peeped a young elephant—
a pink elephant.

"Oh!" said Elmer and Wilbur in surprise.
"Very pretty," Elmer added quickly.
Rose became even pinker.
"She blushes very easily," whispered Eldo.
"I imagine that's why she's called Rose."
"Pleased to meet you," Rose said, and she
blushed again.

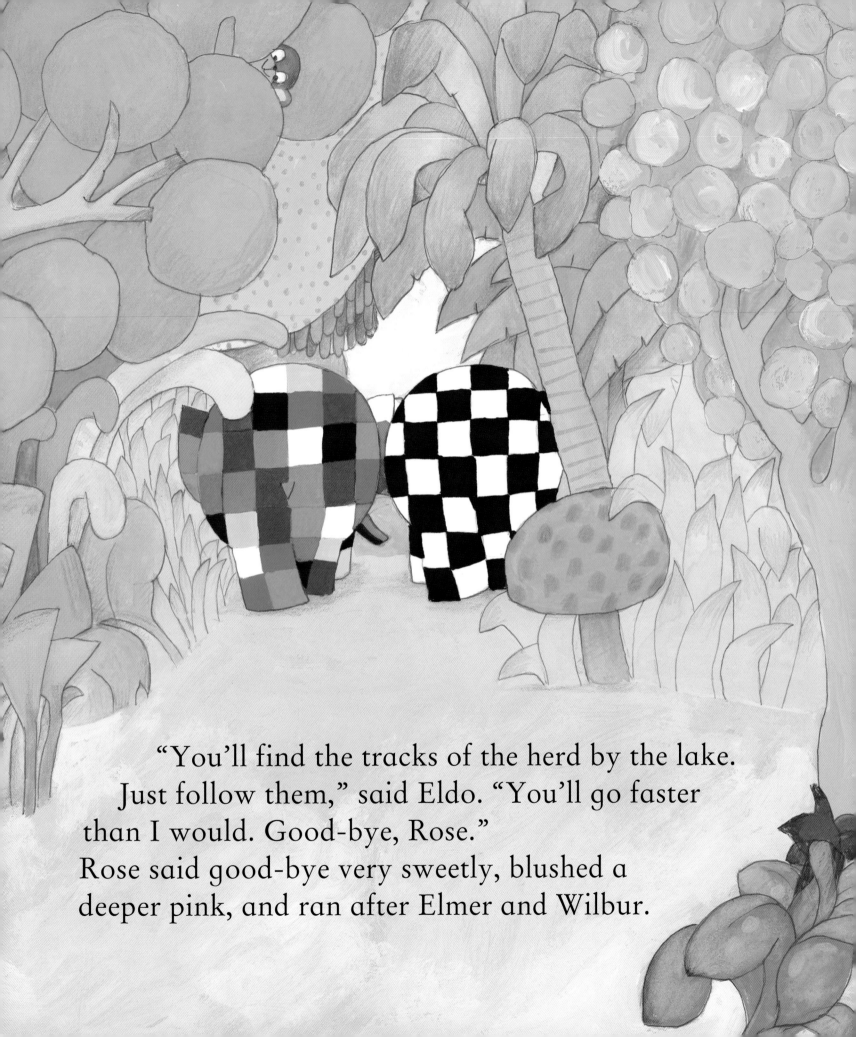

"You'll find the tracks of the herd by the lake.
Just follow them," said Eldo. "You'll go faster
than I would. Good-bye, Rose."
Rose said good-bye very sweetly, blushed a
deeper pink, and ran after Elmer and Wilbur.

At the lake, they met another elephant.
Rose stared and hid between Elmer and Wilbur.
"Hello, Elmer. Hello, Wilbur," said the elephant.
"Hello . . ." he continued awkwardly, looking at Rose.
"Rose," said Elmer helpfully.
After the elephant had gone, Rose said,
"That's a strange one."

Every so often, to make the journey
more fun, they raced one another.

Rose loved that because somehow she always won, and every time, she blushed even pinker.

Between races, Wilbur played tricks with his voice.
He made his voice roar from behind a rock and shout
from a treetop. Rose squealed with excitement, blushed
almost red, and held onto Elmer's trunk.
Elmer just chuckled.

Suddenly Rose said excitedly, "Listen!
They're just over the hill. I'll go alone now.
You may upset the others. They're quite shy.
You're all such unusual elephants, especially
the strange gray one we saw. Thank you for
bringing me back."
"Come and visit us sometime," Elmer called after her.
"Strange gray one? What did she mean?" asked Wilbur.
"I think she was joking," said Elmer.

From the hill, they watched Rose safely join the herd.
"She wasn't joking," said Elmer.
"No wonder she thought the gray elephant was strange."

The elephants in Rose's herd were all . . .

PINK!

Going home, Elmer and Wilbur were met by Eldo.
"You knew about the pink elephants, didn't you,
Grandpa Eldo?" said Elmer.
"Yes, I wanted you to see them," said Eldo.
"Rose was nice," said Wilbur. "I thought she was
unique, and she thought the gray elephant was unique."
"They're probably all nice, unique or not," said Elmer.

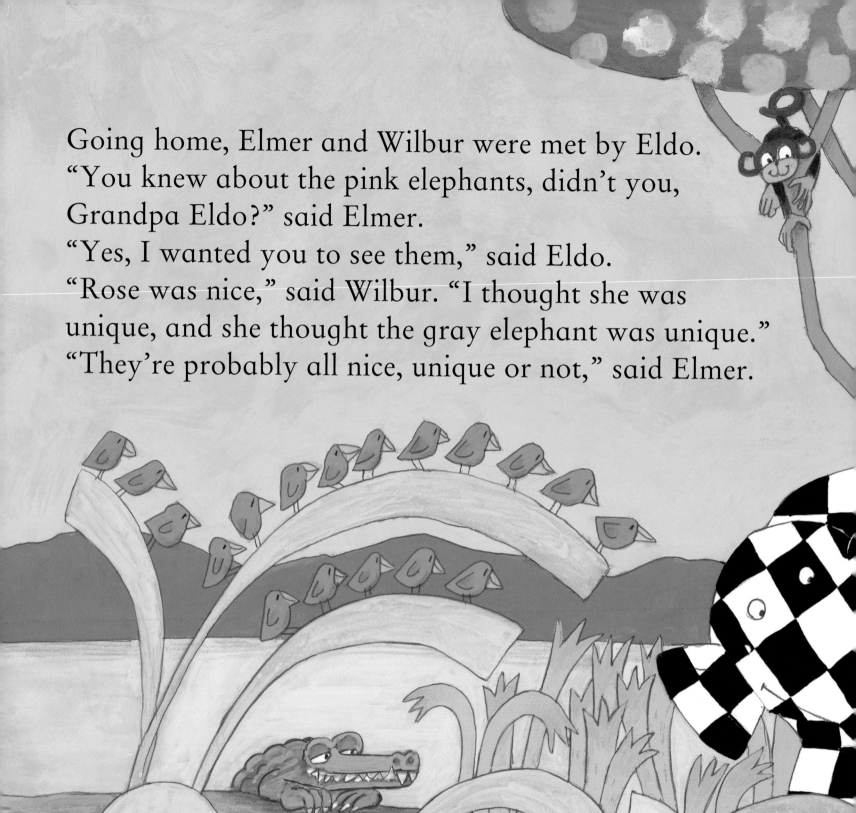

Wilbur grinned. "Remember what you said, Elmer? Imagine a herd like one of us." "Especially like you, Elmer," laughed Eldo. Elmer smiled and said nothing. He was imagining a herd of elephants like himself . . .

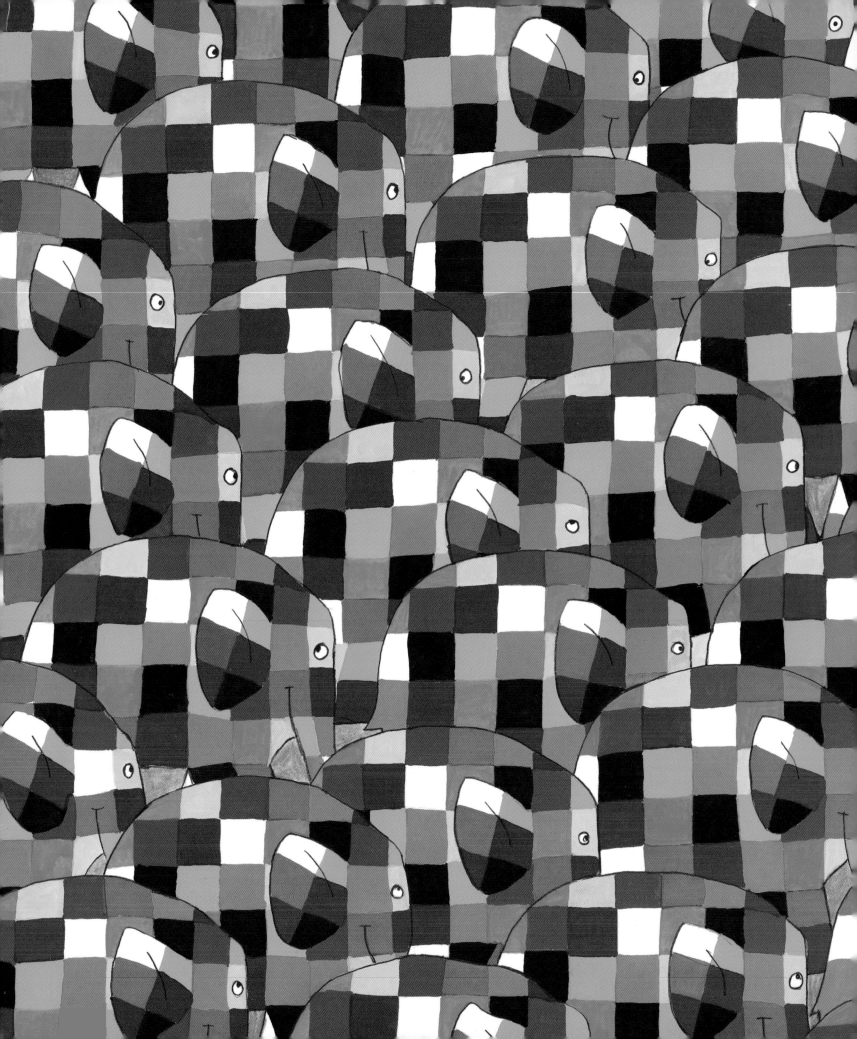